D0513333

Walker Books is grateful for permission to reproduce the following copyright material:

"The Elephant" by Hilaire Belloc (published in *Selected Cautionary Verses*, Puffin 1987) reprinted by permission of the Peters, Fraser and Dunlop Group Ltd.

Acknowledgements:

All the stories in this treasury have been previously published by Walker Books as a self-contained volume, except:

page 30 **"Pit-a-Pat-a-Parrot"** is taken from *Asana and the Animals*.

page 32 **"Nasty Kids, Nice Kids"** is taken from *Kids*.

page 38 **"Elephant Nonsense"** is taken from *I Never Saw a Purple Cow*.

page 44 **"Chi-li the Panda"** is taken from *Baby Animals*.

page 46 **"That's the Way to Do It!"** is taken from *Who's Been Sleeping in My Porridge?*

page 60 **"Paintbox People"** is taken from *Tail Feathers from Mother Goose*, edited by Iona Opie.

page 68 **"Pog had"** is taken from *Pog*.

First published 2000 by Walker Books Ltd, 87 Vauxhall Walk, London SE11 5HJ

10 9 8 7 6 5 4 3 2 1

This book has been typeset in Garamond and Lucy Cousins font.

Printed in Hong Kong

British Library Cataloguing in Publication Data
A catalogue record for this book is available from the British Library.

ISBN 0-7445-6760-2

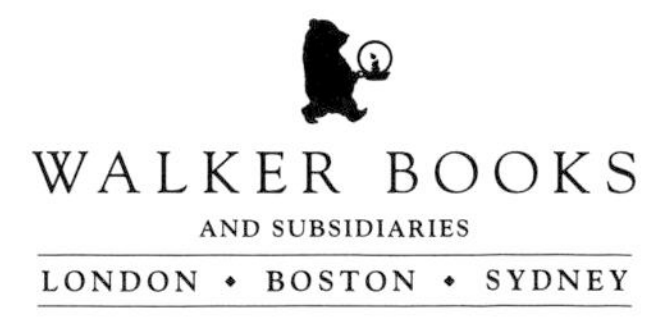
WALKER BOOKS
AND SUBSIDIARIES
LONDON • BOSTON • SYDNEY

Contents

Pog

GINGER

by Charlotte Voake

Ginger was a lucky cat. He lived with a little girl who made him delicious meals and gave him a beautiful basket, where he would curl up … and close his eyes.

Here he is, fast asleep.

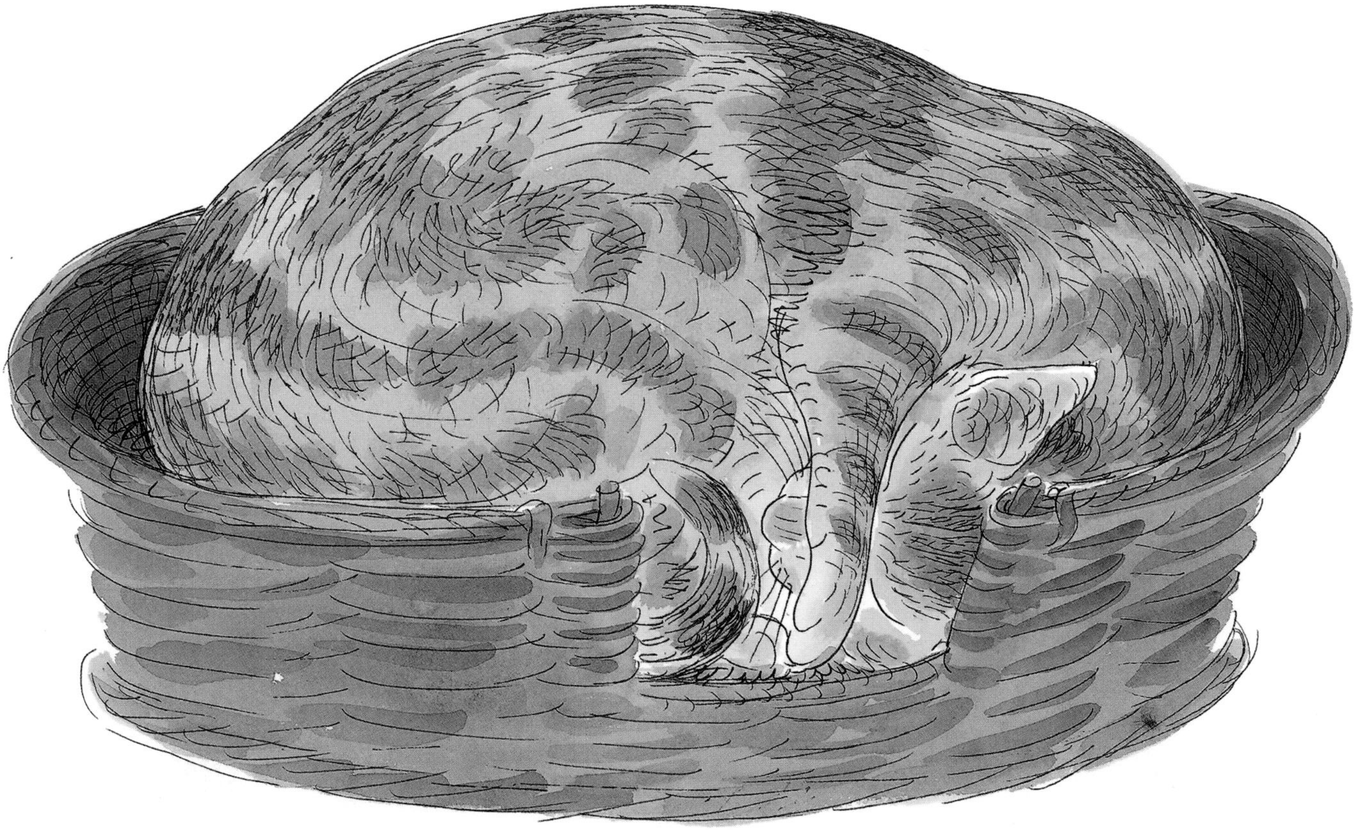

But here he is again, WIDE AWAKE. What's this? A kitten!

"He'll be a nice new friend for you, Ginger," said the little girl. But Ginger didn't want a new friend, especially one like this. Ginger hoped the kitten would go away, but he didn't.

Everywhere Ginger went, the kitten followed, springing out from behind doors, leaping on to Ginger's back, even eating Ginger's food! What a naughty kitten!

But what upset Ginger more than anything was that whenever he got into his beautiful basket, the kitten always climbed in too, and the little girl didn't do anything about it.

So Ginger decided to leave home.

He went out through the cat flap and he didn't come back.

The kitten waited for a bit, then he got into Ginger's basket.

It wasn't the same without Ginger.

The kitten played with some flowers, then he found somewhere to sharpen his claws. The little girl found him on the table drinking some milk. "You naughty kitten!" she said. "I thought you were with Ginger. Where is he anyway?" She looked in Ginger's basket, but of course he wasn't there. "Perhaps he's eating his food," she said. But Ginger wasn't there either. "I hope he's not upset," she said. "I hope he hasn't run away."

She put on her wellingtons and went out into the garden, and that is where she found him; a very wet, sad, cold Ginger, hiding under a bush.

The little girl carried Ginger and the kitten inside. "It's a pity you can't be friends," she said.

She gave Ginger a special meal. She gave the kitten a little plate of his own. Then she tucked Ginger into his own warm basket.

All she could find for the kitten to sleep in was a little tiny cardboard box. But the kitten didn't mind, because cats love cardboard boxes (however small they are).

So when the little girl went in to see the two cats again, THIS is how she found them.

And now Ginger and the naughty kitten get along very well …

most of the time!

Birthday Happy, Contrary Mary

by Anita Jeram

Today was Contrary Mary's birthday.

"Happy Birthday!" said her mum and dad.

"Happy everyday," said Contrary Mary.

She loved the presents her mum and dad gave her.

"Much you very thank!" she said.

Mary tried out her new stilts – upside down. Then she piled her new farm animals into her new spotty cap and said, "This box makes a good hat."

After lunch Mary helped her mum make things for her birthday tea.

She made inside-out Swiss cheese sandwiches and iced all the little fairy cakes upside down.

Then she went upstairs to put on her party clothes.

"Come in," Mary's dad said to her friends when they arrived for the party. "We're playing hide-and-seek."

It wasn't hard to find Mary. They played hide-and-seek again and again and Mary was always the one found first.

When they played musical bumps and everyone was dancing to the music,

Contrary Mary sat on the floor. Then, when the music stopped and everyone flopped to the floor, Contrary Mary danced.

At teatime, everyone loved the inside-out sandwiches and got icing on their

chins eating the fairy cakes. Contrary Mary ate her jelly with a knife and fork and everyone copied her.

Mary's mum brought out her birthday cake.

"Happy birthday to you!" everyone sang. But Contrary Mary did not look happy, not one bit.

Then Contrary Mary's dad had an idea. He sang:

"You to birthday, happy
You to birthday, happy
Mary Contrary,
birthday happy
You to birthday, happy!"

Contrary Mary laughed and blew out her candles and everyone shouted,

"Birthday Happy,
Contrary Mary!"

Za-Za's Baby Brother

by Lucy Cousins

My mum is going to have a baby. She has a big fat tummy. There's not much room for a cuddle.

Granny came to look after me. Dad took Mum to the hospital.

When the baby was born
we went to see Mum.

When Mum came home
she was very tired. I had
to be very quiet and help
Dad look after her.

All my uncles and aunts
came to see the baby.
I played on my own.

Dad was always busy.
Mum was always busy.
"Mum, will you read
me a story?"
"Later, Za-za."

"Dad, will you read me a story?"

"Not now, Za-za. We're going shopping soon."

"Mum, can we go to the toyshop?"

"Sorry, Za-za, baby's hungry and we have to go home."

"Can I have **my** tea soon?"

"Yes, Za-za."

"Mum! I want a cuddle **now!**"

waah waah waah

"Why don't you cuddle the baby?"

So I cuddled the baby ...
and I pushed him ...
and I built a tower.

He was nice. It was fun.

When the baby got tired
Mum put him to bed. Then I got
my cuddle ... and a
bedtime story.

by Phyllis Root
illustrated by Helen Craig

One Tuesday Bonnie Bumble baked six plum turnovers for breakfast. "Delicious," she said, and she ate up five, every bite. There wasn't even a crumb left over for her little dog, Spot.

But when Bonnie Bumble got up from her chair,
she turned over
upside down.

And nothing
could turn her
back over
again.

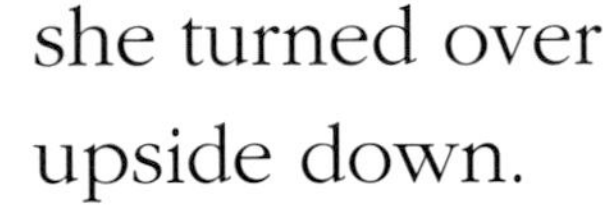

So Bonnie Bumble put her hat on her feet and her shoes on her hands. Then she went to do her chores.

Upside down she milked the cow.
But the milk SPLASHED out of the bucket.

Upside down she gathered the eggs. But the eggs SMASHED out of the basket.

On the way back to the house, the sheep nibbled her hair. And the pig's tail tickled her ear.

"This will never do!" said Bonnie Bumble.

Back into the kitchen she went to find the last plum turnover. Upside down she ate it, almost every bite.

When she got up from the table, she turned back over, right side up! "Thank goodness everything's back to normal," said Bonnie Bumble. And it was ...

except for Spot, who had eaten up all the crumbs.

Baby Duck and the New Eyeglasses

by **Amy Hest**
illustrated by
Jill Barton

Baby Duck was looking in the mirror. She was trying on her new eyeglasses. They were too big on her baby face. They pushed against her baby cheeks. And she did not look like Baby.

Baby came slowly down the stairs.

"Park time!" said Mr Duck. "Grandpa will be waiting in his boat at the lake!"

"How sweet you look in your new eyeglasses!" cooed Mrs Duck. "Don't you love them?"

"No," Baby said.

"How well you must see in your new eyeglasses!" clucked Mr Duck. "Don't you like them just a little?"

"No," Baby said.

The Duck family went out of the front door. Mr and Mrs Duck hopped along. "Hop down the lane, Baby!"

Baby did not hop. Her glasses might fall off.

Mr and Mrs Duck danced along.

"Dance down the lane, Baby!"

Baby did not dance. Her glasses might fall off.

When they got to the park, Baby sat in the grass behind a tree. She sang a little song.

"Poor, poor Baby, she looks ugly
In her bad eyeglasses.
Everyone can play but me,
Poor, poor, poor, poor Baby."

Grandpa came up the hill. "Where's that Baby?" he called.

"I'm afraid she is hiding," Mrs Duck sighed.

"She does not like her new eyeglasses," worried Mr Duck.

Grandpa sat in the grass behind the tree. "I like your hiding place," he whispered.

"Thank you," Baby said.

Grandpa peered round the side of the tree. "I see new eyeglasses," he whispered. "Are they blue?"

"No," Baby said.

"Green?" Grandpa whispered.

"No," Baby said.

"Cocoa brown?" Grandpa whispered.

Baby came out from behind the tree.

Grandpa folded his arms. "Well," he said, "I think those eyeglasses are *very* fine."

"Why?" Baby asked.

"Because they are red like mine!" Grandpa said.

Grandpa kissed Baby's cheek. "Can you still run to the lake and splash about?"

Baby ran and splashed. Then she splashed harder. Her glasses did not fall off.

"Can you still twirl three times without falling down?"

Baby twirled. One, two, three. She did not fall down. And her glasses did not fall off.

"Come with me, Baby. I have a surprise," Grandpa said.

They walked down to the pier. Grandpa's boat was bobbing on the water. There was another boat, too.

"Can you read what it says?" Grandpa asked.

Baby read, "B-a-b-y."

The letters were very clear. Then Grandpa and Mr and Mrs Duck sat in Grandpa's boat.

But Baby sat in *her* boat and
sang a new song.

"I have nice new eyeglasses!
I look like my grandpa.
My rowing-boat is lots of fun,
And I can read my name on it."

BEANS ON TOAST

Beans on stalks

Beans on legs

Beans on racks

Beans on wheels

Beans on the road

Beans on cranes

Beans on the boil

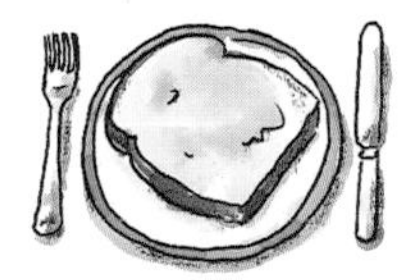

by Paul Dowling

Beans
on tins

Beans on
trucks

Beans on shelves

Beans on
the counter

Beans on the
way home

Beans on
cooker

Beans on
spoon

Beans
on head

Beans
on floor

Beans on toast

CALAMITY

James and Horatio were building a tower.

"One, two, three," said James as he balanced the blocks.

"Seven, four," added Horatio.

"HEE-HAW!" BUMP! Something crashed into the Useful Box and sent everything flying.

"What was that?" asked Horatio.

"It's a calamity," said James, looking at the mess.

"What were you doing, Calamity?" asked Horatio.

"Racing," Calamity said. "And I won."

"Can I race?" asked Horatio.

"Find yourself a jockey," Calamity said. "Here's mine." She turned round.

But that's a bobbin, thought James. He started to tidy up.

by Camilla Ashforth

Horatio looked for a jockey. I like this one, he thought. It was James's clock.

"Are you ready?" asked Calamity.

They waited a moment.

"One, two, three, go!" Calamity called. She hurtled round the Useful Box. Twice.

Horatio tried to move his jockey.

He pushed it and pulled it. Then he rolled it over. His jockey would not budge.

Calamity screeched to a halt. "Hee-haw! I won!" she bellowed. "Let's race again."

James turned round. He picked up Horatio's jockey.

"That's my clock," said James and he put it in his Useful Box.

Horatio looked for another jockey.

“One, two, three, go!” Calamity called. She galloped very fast. Backwards and forwards.

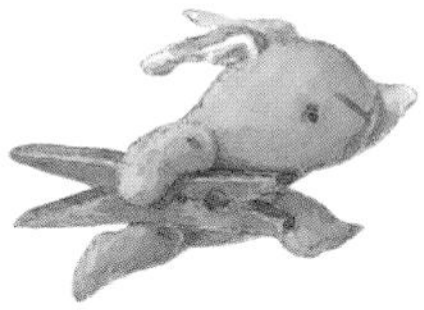

Horatio looked around. I’ll go this way, he thought, and he set off with his new jockey.

“Hee-haw! Won again!” cried Calamity, stopping suddenly.

Horatio looked puzzled.

“One more race,” Calamity said. “I’m good at this.”

“James,” whispered Horatio, “can you help me win this time?”

“What you need is a race track,” said James. “I’ll make you one. This block is the start,” he said. “And this string is the finishing line. Ready, steady, go!”

Calamity thundered off. She was going the wrong way.

Horatio headed for the finishing line as fast as he could.

Calamity turned in a circle and headed back towards James.

"Stop!"
James cried.

As Horatio crossed the line,
Calamity collided with the Useful Box. CRASH!

"That was a good race. Who won?" asked Calamity.

"I think you both did," James said, and squeezed Horatio tight.

Pit-a-Pat-a-Parrot

by Grace Nichols
illustrated by Sarah Adams

Pit-a-pat-a-parrot
on her parrot back
pit a little pat a little
don't forget to scratch
a little
don't forget to chat
a little
she will learn the knack
a little

If you pit-a-pat-a-parrot
if you chit-a-chat-a-parrot
while you scritch and scratch a parrot

She will chit and chat right back.

Nasty Kids, Nice Kids

What are nasty kids like?

They pull your hair,
they call you names,

They tell you lies,
they spoil your games,

They draw on walls,
scream on the floor.

Nasty kids want more, more, more.

by Catherine and Laurence Anholt

What are nice kids like?

They make you laugh,
they hold your hand,

Nice kids always
understand.

They share their toys,
they let you play,

They chase the nasty kids **away.**

Grandad's Magic

by Bob Graham

Three dogs lived in Alison's house. Two sat high on the shelf. They were very precious to Alison's mum. They were very breakable. Alison was not to touch them even if she could reach. She didn't like them anyway.

Alison much preferred Rupert. He lived on the armchair. Rupert only left the chair to have his dinner or go to the toilet. He wouldn't leave the chair for Alison's mum *or* her dad, and certainly not for Max, who often tried to pull his tail.

Rupert wouldn't even get out of his chair when Grandma and Grandad came to lunch on Sunday. Alison held Max for Grandma to kiss. He curled his fists and kicked his legs.

"Give him to me," said Grandad. "I know how to handle this young chap. Now for my magic..."

Grandad reached into Max's shirt and slowly pulled out a chocolate bear.

"Have you been keeping that in your shirt all this time?" he said. Max's face lit up with pleasure. Then Grandad lost the bear ... and found it again under Rupert's collar!

"It's magic," said Alison.

"Watch me, Grandad," said Alison. She had a trick of her own. She was learning to juggle with three puffins filled with sand that Grandad had given her. This *sounded* easy, but she

had to keep them going from hand to hand. The idea was to have three puffins in the air all at once.

"Try one at a time, Alison," said Grandad. "Backwards and forwards, and when you

learn that, try two, and when you learn that, try three."

"I'm not as good as I used to be," said Grandad.

Sunday was the only day the china dogs came down from the shelf. Alison's mum used them as a table decoration. They guarded the fruit. Every Sunday Grandad picked his table napkin out of the air like an apple off a tree. And he talked of his best trick of all …

"I used to be able to take this tablecloth, give it a pull in a certain kind of way, and it would whip out from under all this stuff and leave everything standing there. But that was a long time ago."

Then one Sunday, Grandad noticed how well Alison juggled, and …

without warning, he removed his coat and climbed on to the chair.

"One good trick deserves another," he said. And he gave the tablecloth a short, snapping tug.

There was a moment of silence. Mum looked pale.

"You did it!" said Alison.

Grandad did a triumphant dance round the room. And *that's* when it happened.

An orange rolled off the bowl, hit one of the precious dogs and sent it spinning into mid-air … just as Rupert happened to be making a trip to the toilet. It settled on his very broad back …

then landed safely in Max's lap. Alison held her breath. Would Grandad get into trouble? But Mum smiled thinly as she put the dogs back on the shelf.

"Don't *you* try that trick, Ally," said Grandad.

The following Sunday there were a number of changes in Alison's house. When Grandma and Grandad came to lunch, the dogs stayed on the shelf. And the table was set with unbreakable plastic plates and place mats.

Just before lunch, Rupert found a box of chocolates hidden under his cushion.

Later, Grandad made the chocolates appear just like magic. They were for Mum, who had such a shock last week.

Alison was dismayed. "That's not magic, it's a trick! You put them there, Grandad. The price is still on them!"

"We performers can't get it right all the time, Alison," Grandad said, "but the chocolates have certainly vanished.

Now let's see how long *you* can spin this plastic plate on the end of your finger!"

Elephant Nonsense

THE ELEPHANT IS A GRACEFUL BIRD

The elephant is a graceful bird;
It flits from twig to twig.
It builds its nest in a rhubarb tree
And whistles like a pig.

Anonymous

WAY DOWN SOUTH

Way down South where bananas grow,
A grasshopper stepped on an elephant's toe.
The elephant said, with tears in his eyes,
"Pick on somebody your own size."

Anonymous

illustrated by Emma Chichester Clark

THE ELEPHANT

When people call this beast to mind,
They marvel more and more
At such a LITTLE tail behind,
So LARGE a trunk before.

Hilaire Belloc

The Teeny Tiny WOMAN

A Traditional Tale

illustrated by Arthur Robins

Once upon a time a teeny tiny woman who lived in a teeny tiny house put on her teeny tiny hat and went out for a teeny tiny walk.

When the teeny tiny woman had gone a teeny tiny way, she went through a teeny tiny gate into a teeny tiny churchyard.

In the teeny tiny churchyard the teeny tiny woman found a teeny tiny bone on a teeny tiny grave. Then the teeny tiny woman said to her teeny tiny self, "This teeny tiny bone will make some teeny tiny soup for my teeny tiny supper."

So the teeny tiny woman took the teeny tiny bone back to her teeny tiny house. When she got home she felt a teeny tiny tired, so she put the teeny tiny bone in her teeny tiny cupboard and got into her teeny tiny bed for a teeny tiny sleep.

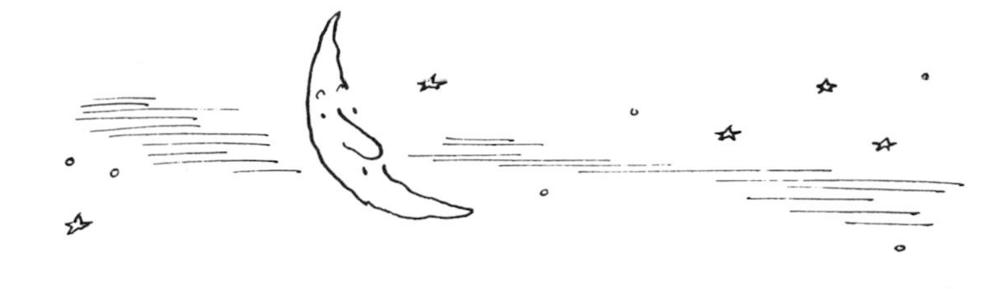

After a teeny tiny while the teeny tiny woman was woken by a teeny tiny voice that said, "Give me my bone!"

The teeny tiny woman was a teeny tiny frightened, so she hid her teeny tiny head under her teeny tiny sheet.

The teeny tiny voice said a teeny tiny closer and a teeny tiny louder, **"Give me my bone!"**

This made the teeny tiny woman a teeny tiny more frightened, so she hid her teeny tiny head a teeny tiny further under her teeny tiny sheet.

Then the teeny tiny voice said a teeny tiny closer and a teeny tiny louder, **"Give me my bone!"**

The teeny tiny woman was a teeny tiny more frightened, but she put her teeny tiny head out from under her teeny tiny sheet and said in her **loudest** teeny tiny voice …

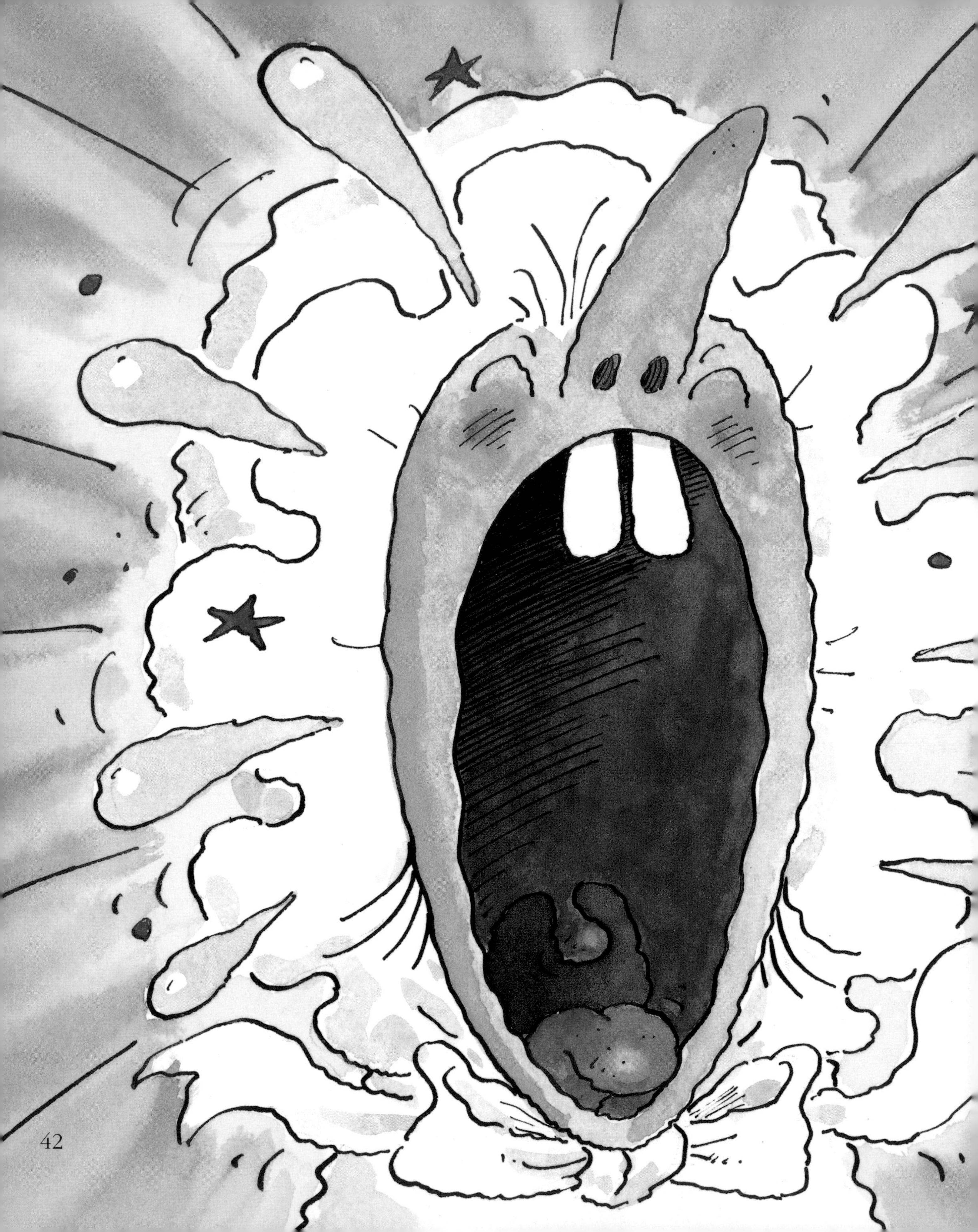

"TAKE
IT!"

Chi-li the Panda

by Derek Hall • illustrated by John Butler

Chi-li loves to play with his mother. Sometimes she gives him a piggy-back and then he feels as tall as a grown-up panda.

Soon, it is dinner time. The grown-ups eat lots of bamboo shoots, crunching the juicy stems. Chi-li likes to chew the soft leaves.

The grown-ups eat for such a long time, they always fall asleep afterwards. Chi-li scampers off to play. He rolls over and over in the snow and tumbles down a hill.

When Chi-li stops at the bottom he cannot see his mother any more. But he sees a leopard! Chi-li is very frightened.

He scrambles over to the nearest tree and climbs up. Chi-li has never climbed before, and it is so easy! He digs his claws into the bark and goes up and up.

Soon, he is near the top. Chi-li feels so good up here. And he can see such a long way over the mountains and trees and snow of China.

Chi-li hears his mother crying. She is looking for him. He starts to climb down. But going down is harder than climbing up, and he slips. Plop! He lands in the snow.

Chi-li's mother is so happy. She gathers him up in her big furry arms and cuddles him. It is lovely to be warm and safe with her again.

That's the Way to Do It!

by Colin McNaughton

There was an old woman
Who lived in a shoe,
She had so many children
She didn't know what to do;
So she sought the advice
Of her friend Mr Punch,
Who said fry them with onions
And eat them for lunch!

Friends by Kim Lewis

Sam's friend Alice came to play on the farm. They were in the garden when they heard loud clucking coming from the hen house.

"Listen!" said Sam. "That means a hen has laid an egg."

"An egg!" said Alice. "Let's go and find it."

Sam and Alice ran to the hen house.

"Look," said Alice. "There's the egg!"

"I can put it in my hat," said Sam.

"I can put your hat in my bucket,"

said Alice, "and put the bucket in the wheelbarrow."

"Then we can take it home," said Sam.

The geese stood across the path.

"I'm afraid of geese," said Alice.

"Come on," said Sam. "We can go the long way round."

Alice pushed the wheelbarrow through the trees.

"It's my turn now," said Sam, and he pulled it through the long grass and thistles.

Together, they lifted it over a ditch.

Sam and Alice went into the barn. They were followed by Glen, the old farm dog.

"Is the egg all right?" asked Alice.

Sam and Alice looked in the hat. The egg was safe and smooth, without a crack.

"Look what we've found!" said Alice, holding out the egg to Glen.

"No!" cried Sam. "He'll eat it!"

Sam reached out to take the egg.

Alice held it tight.

"It's mine!" said Sam.

"It's not!" said Alice. "I found it!"

"They're my hens!" said Sam, pushing Alice.

Just then loud clucking came from the hen house. Sam ran out of the barn.

"Another egg!" he cried.

Sam and Alice looked at each other.

"We can go and find it," said Sam.

"Yes, let's!" said Alice, and smiled.

SMASH went the egg as it fell on the ground. Glen started to eat it.

"I don't like you any more," said Alice. She picked up her bucket and went out of the barn.

Sam put on his empty hat. He did like Alice and he didn't like Alice and he felt he was going to cry.

Sam put the egg in his hat. He gave the hat to Alice who put it in her bucket. They tiptoed past the geese and Glen and walked back to the house.

"What have you two been doing?" asked Mum.

"Finding eggs," said Sam.

"Together!" said Alice.

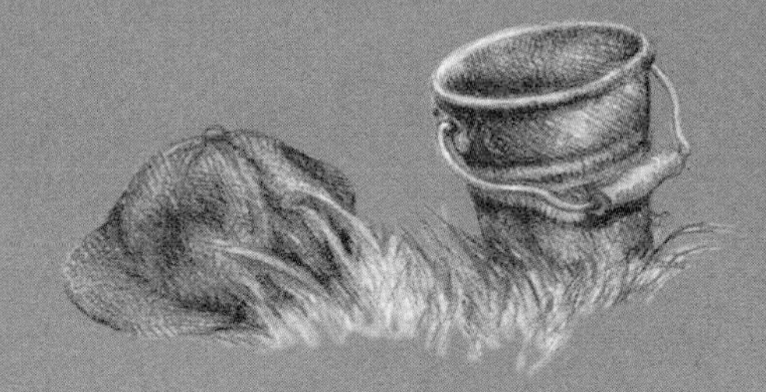

Mimi and the Blackberry Pies

by Martin Waddell illustrated by Leo Hartas

Mimi lived with her mouse sisters and brothers beneath the big tree. It was blackberry time in the hedge.

"I'm going to make blackberry pies," Mimi told her mouse sisters.

"We'll help you, Mimi!" her mouse sisters said. "We'll pick the best berries to go in the pies!" They all loved Mimi's blackberry pies.

Mimi's mouse sisters took their baskets out to the hedge, and they started to pick the juicy blackberries, but the berries were nice and they ate a lot more than they picked.

They ate

and they ate

and they ate

and they ate

and they ate

and they ate. But they didn't pick many berries for Mimi.

"This isn't much help!" Mimi said, when she'd counted the berries they'd picked.

"We'll help you, Mimi," her mouse brothers cried. "We'll pick trillions of berries!" They all loved Mimi's blackberry pies.

Mimi's mouse brothers climbed up into the hedge and got busy. But soon some-brother-mouse splatted some-other-brother-mouse with a berry! Mouse-brother-splatting looked fun. They forgot all about picking berries for Mimi, and started mouse-splatting each other instead.

They splatted

and they splatted

and they splatted

and they splatted

and they splatted.

But they didn't pick many berries for Mimi.

"This isn't much help!" Mimi sighed. And she went out to the hedge and picked all the berries she needed herself.

Mimi made blackberry pies. A sweet berry smell drifted over Mimi's sisters and brothers.

Their noses twitched

and they twitched

and they twitched

and they twitched

and they twitched.

The rich berry smell was so good that Mimi's sisters and brothers ran to her house. Mimi came out with the pies that she'd made on a tray. Mimi's blackberry pies were bursting with berries and juice.

"This time I'm sure that you'll help!" Mimi said. And her mouse sisters and brothers helped Mimi eat all her blackberry pies!

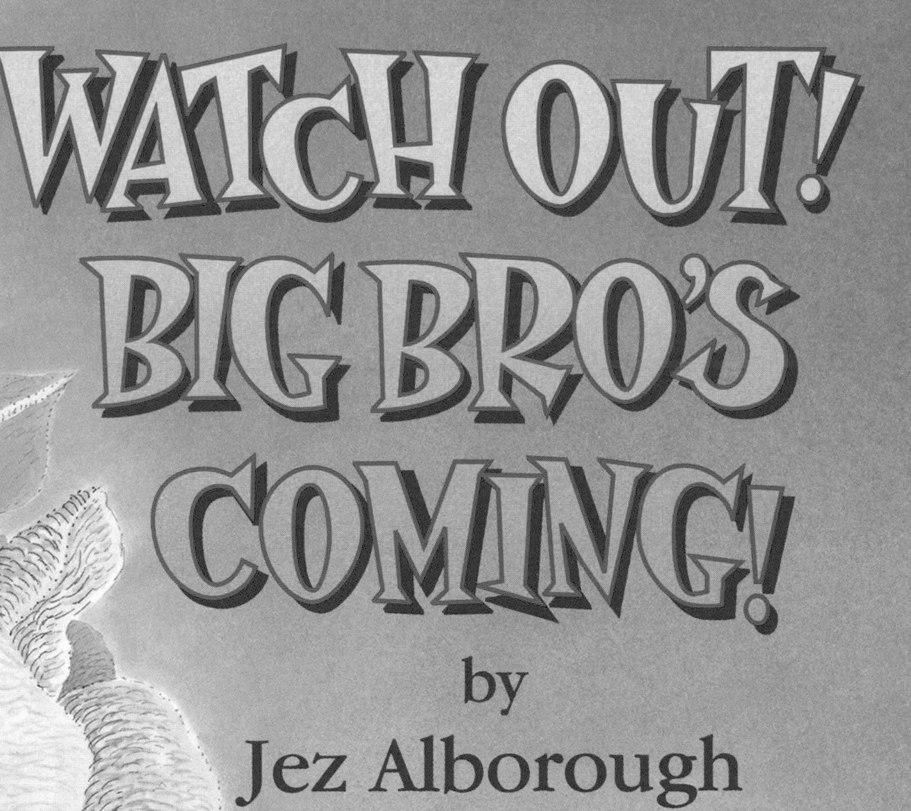

WATCH OUT! BIG BRO'S COMING!

by

Jez Alborough

"Help!" squeaked a mouse. "He's coming!"

"Who's coming?" asked a frog.

"Big Bro," said the mouse. "He's rough, he's tough, and he's big."

"Big?" said the frog. "How big?"

The mouse stretched out his arms as wide as they could go. "This big," he cried, and he scampered off to hide.

"Look out!" croaked the frog. "Big Bro's coming!"

"Big who?" asked the parrot.

"Big Bro," said the frog. "He's rough, he's tough, and he's really big."

"Really big?" said the parrot. "How big?"

The frog stretched out his arms as wide as they could go. "This big," he cried, and he hopped off to hide.

"Watch out!" squawked the parrot. "Big Bro's coming!"

"Who's he?" asked the chimpanzee.

"Don't you know Big Bro?" asked the parrot. "He's rough, he's tough, and he's ever so big."

"Ever so big?" said the chimpanzee. "How big?"

The parrot stretched out his wings as wide as they could go. "This big," he cried, and he flapped off to hide.

"Ooh-ooh! Look out!" whooped the chimpanzee. "Big Bro's coming!"

"Big Joe?" said the elephant.

"No," said the chimpanzee. "Big Bro. He's rough, he's tough, and everybody knows how big Big Bro is."

The elephant shook his head. "I don't," he said.

The chimpanzee stretched out his arms as wide as they could go. "This big," he cried.

"That big?" gulped the elephant. "Let's hide!"

So there they all were, hiding and waiting, waiting and hiding.

"Where is he?" asked the elephant.

"Shhh," said the chimpanzee. "I don't know."

"Why don't you creep out and have a look around?" whispered the elephant.

"Not me," said the chimpanzee.

"Not me," said the parrot.

"Not me," said the frog.

"All right," said the mouse. "As you're all so frightened, I'll go."

The mouse tiptoed ever so slowly out from his hiding place. He looked this way and that way to see if he could see Big Bro.

And then … "He's coming!" shrieked the mouse.

"H … h … h … hide!"

Big Bro came closer and closer and closer. Everyone covered their eyes.

"Oh no," whispered the frog.

"Help," gasped the parrot.

"I can hear something coming," whined the chimpanzee.

"It's him," whimpered the elephant. "*It's … it's …*"

"BIG BRO!" shrieked the mouse.

"Is that Big Bro?" asked the frog.

"He's tiny," said the parrot.

"Teeny weeny," said the chimpanzee.

"He's a mouse," said the elephant.

Big Bro looked up at them all, took a deep breath, and said …

"BOO!"

"Come on,
Little Bro," said
Big Bro. "Mum wants you back home ***now!***"

"Wow," said the elephant.

"Phew," said the chimpanzee.

"He is rough," said the parrot.

"And tough," said the frog.

"Rough and tough," said Little Bro, looking back over his shoulder.

"And I *told* you he was big!"

Oh, Tucker!

by Steven Kroll
illustrated by Scott Nash

"**TUCKER!** Time for breakfast!" Tina called.

Tucker came running. **WHAM!** He knocked over a dustbin.

He jumped up and licked Tina's chin.

"Oh, Tucker!" Tina giggled.

Tucker pushed open the front door and raced into the house. **WHAM!** He knocked over a vase of flowers. **WHAM!** He knocked a china plate on to the floor.

"Oh, Tucker!" Tina groaned.

Tucker ran for the stairs.

"Tucker, no!" Tina cried. "It's breakfast-time!"

But Tucker didn't listen. He had to say good morning to Tina's parents. He bounded up the stairs.

Mum and Dad were fast asleep. Tucker didn't mind. **WHAM!** He landed on the bed.

"OOF!" said Mum.
"OOF!" said Dad.

Tucker licked their faces and wagged his tail. **WHAM!** He knocked over the bedside lamp. **WHAM!** He knocked over the clock and the radio and a glass of water.

"Oh, Tucker!" said Tina.

Tucker barked. He ran back to the stairs – and slipped!

Tucker flew through the air.

WHAM! He hit the wall and a picture fell. He scrambled to his feet. **WHAM!** He knocked over a table and a lamp. The lampshade plopped on his head.

Tucker couldn't see but that didn't stop him. He zigzagged through the living room.

"Oh, Tucker, WAIT!" Tina cried.

But Tucker didn't listen.

WHAM! He knocked over a chair. **WHAM!** He knocked over a vase. **WHAM!** He knocked over a plant and a bowl and a china cat.

Tucker stepped on Tina's skateboard and zoomed down the hall! Tina hid her eyes. "Oh, Tucker!"

WHAM! He crashed against the kitchen sink. The lampshade flew off his head. Tina hurried in. Mum and Dad hurried in, too.

"Here, Tucker, look," Tina said. She set his dish down in front of him. They all held their breath. Tucker dug in.

"Finally," said Tina.

Mum and Dad sighed with relief. Tina smiled. Such a nice dog. Such a friendly dog. Who could possibly scold him?

WHAM!
WHAM!
WHAM!
WHAM!
WHAM!
WHAM!
WHAM!

"Oh, Tucker!"

PAINTBOX PEOPLE

illustrated by ***Nicola Bayley***

Mrs Red she went to bed with a turban on her head.

Mrs White had a fright in the middle of the night;
Saw a ghost eating toast halfway up a lamppost.

Mrs Brown went to town with her knickers hanging down;
Mrs Green saw the scene and put it in a magazine.

A Friend for Little Bear

by Harry Horse

Little Bear lived all alone on a desert island. "I wish I had something to play with," he said.

A stick came floating by. Little Bear picked it out of the sea. He drew a picture in the sand. Then he drew some more. "I need something else to play with," he said. He was tired of drawing pictures.

A bottle came floating by. Little Bear picked it out of the sea. He filled it up with water, then poured out the water on the sand.

"I need a cup," said Little Bear, "to pour the water into."

Then something spotted came floating by. Little Bear wondered what it was. "It isn't a cup," he said, but he pulled it out of the sea anyway. It was a wooden horse.

The wooden horse ran round the island. Little Bear ran after him. The wooden horse hid. Little Bear looked for him. They had a lovely time. They drew pictures in the sand and filled the bottle again and again. They played all day long and then went to sleep under the tall palm tree.

Little Bear woke up. He rubbed his eyes. "Look!" he cried. "Lots of things floating in the water!" He stretched with his stick and pulled out as many as he could. "I don't know what these things are," he said, "but I need them, all the same." He piled them into a heap. Then he sighed. "I still do wish I had a cup."

There wasn't much room on the island now. Little Bear had filled it up. He told the wooden horse to get out of the way. "Climb on to that," said Little Bear. "I need more room for these boxes."

"Look!" cried Little Bear. "A cup!"

SNAP!

The roof broke. The wooden horse fell into the sea and floated away.

Little Bear was filling his bottle with water and pouring the water into his cup. "Watch me!" he cried. He filled up the bottle again. "Watch me!" But no one was there. He looked up. He put the bottle down. He walked all round the island. "Where are you?" he called. "I need you!" but no one answered.

"I need my *friend*," said Little Bear. "I don't need that cup!" He threw all his things back into the sea and they floated away.

He sat underneath the tall palm tree and began to cry.

Little Bear dried his eyes. Then he rubbed them. Something spotted was floating by.

He ran and pulled it out of the sea.

"I only need you, Wooden Horse," he said, and the two of them danced for joy on the sand.

THE RED FOX MONSTER

by ALAN BARON

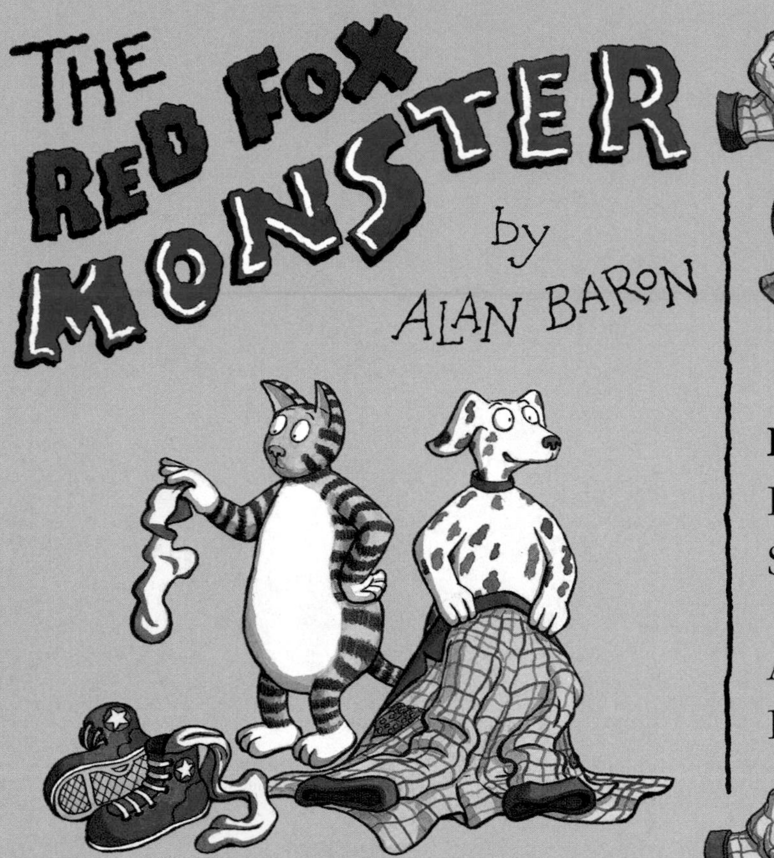

Dan Dog and Tabby Cat were walking by the lake. On the bank they found Red Fox's clothes.

"I've got an idea," said Dan Dog.

They took Red Fox's clothes and put them on. Dan Dog rubbed dirt on his face then jumped on to Tabby Cat's shoulders. The Red Fox Monster hid behind a bush, and waited.

Along came Little Pig. Out jumped the Red Fox Monster shouting, **"Dinnertime!"**

"Help, it's Red Fox!" shouted Little Pig. She turned and ran away.

Along came Lucy Goose, Big Duck and Fat Hen.

Out jumped the Red Fox Monster shouting, **"Dinnertime!"**

"Help, it's Red Fox!" shouted Lucy Goose, Big Duck and Fat Hen. They turned and ran away.

Along came Red Fox.
Out jumped the Red Fox Monster shouting, **"Dinnertime!"**

Red Fox stared at the Red Fox Monster and the Red Fox Monster stared back.

Then Red Fox gave a great big yell. **"Help, it's Red Fox!"** And he turned and ran and jumped back into the lake. Red Fox swam away fast, then stopped.

"Wait a minute!" he shouted. **"You're not Red Fox, I'm Red Fox!"**

Dan Dog and Tabby Cat threw off Red Fox's clothes.

"Time to go!" said Dan Dog.
"Good idea!" said Tabby Cat.
And they went.

Pog had

by Peter Haswell

Pog had a banana. "I wonder what a banana does," said Pog.

He put it on his head. It fell off.

He dropped it on the floor.

It didn't bounce.

He put it in a vase.

It didn't grow.

Pog peeled the banana.

He threw away the skin.

Pog walked…

“Now I know what a banana does,” said Pog.

“It makes you fall down!”

What Newt Could Do for Turtle

Written by
Jonathan London

Illustrated by
Louise Voce

Spring had come to the swamp.

A red-spotted newt crawled out from his winter bed in the mud.

"Help!" cried Newt. "I'm stuck!"

A painted turtle yawned, greeting the spring.

"Coming, dear Newt!" cried Turtle.

Pock! went the mud as Turtle pulled Newt free.

"Thanks, Turtle! You're the best!"

"That's what friends are for!" said Turtle.

"Yep," said Newt. His spots turned a deeper red, and he wondered, *What can I do for Turtle?*

That spring the swamp buzzed with life. There were catfish and dragonflies, cat's-tails and dogwoods, polecats and tadpoles.

Turtle took good care of Newt, and Newt and Turtle were happy just to be together.

But sometimes, when Newt sat alone on his thinking rock, he wondered, *What can I do for Turtle?*

In the summer Newt and Turtle played in their favourite swimming holes.

They swooshed down muddy banks and crashed into the water together – *splash!*

Playing hide-and-seek, Newt climbed on to Turtle's back.

"*Yoo-hoo!* Turtle! Where are you?"

He thought he was on a rock.

"*Boo!*" said Turtle, poking his head out.

Newt jumped high into the air.

Autumn came and the leaves of the swamp trees sailed down like little umbrellas.

One day, Newt was paddling a leaf when an alligator glided up to him.

Turtle was watching but he was so scared he hit the water with a great *smack!* and went under.

Alligator turned her head to look, and at that moment Newt dived away.

One day, a cottonmouth snake slithered off a branch and whispered through the water. Snake swam straight towards Newt.

He was about to strike when Newt heard Turtle's voice,

"*Newt! A snake!*"

Newt plunged into the water and hid at the bottom of the swamp.

Once again, Newt wondered, *What can I do for Turtle?*

Newt and Turtle hid together beneath the duckweed. Newt sighed, happy to be alive, and his spots turned redder. Now, more than ever, he wondered, *What can I do for Turtle?*

Then, one day, a curious bobcat slunk through the reeds, twitched his whiskers and *pounced* – right on to Turtle's back.

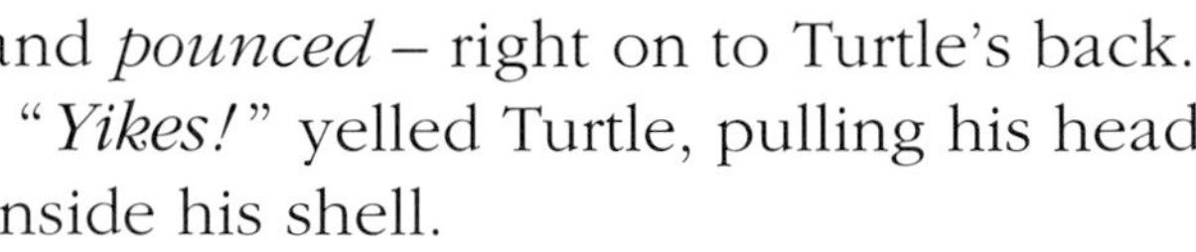

"*Yikes!*" yelled Turtle, pulling his head inside his shell.

Bobcat batted with his paws and flipped Turtle over. Then he grew bored and trotted back into the forest.

Poor Turtle wriggled back and forth. If he could not roll over, he would dry up and die!

"Newt, oh Newt!" he cried. "Where are you?"

Now, across the swamp, Newt was dreaming that Turtle was in trouble. "*What can I do for Turtle?*" he said.

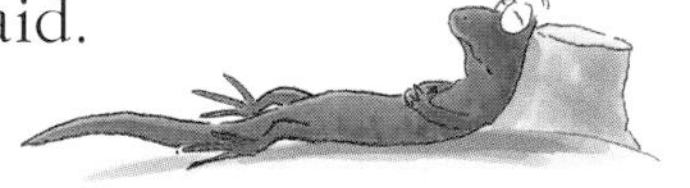

His own words woke him up! His heart bumped and stumbled, just like his feet. He scurried to and fro, searching for his friend.

At last, beneath a weeping willow, Newt found him.

"Turtle!" cried Newt. "What are you doing?"

"Pretending I'm a bowl of soup. *What does it look like I'm doing?*"

"Don't worry," said Newt. "I'll help you."

This was his big chance! Newt went to his thinking rock, and thought and thought.

"*Aha!*" he said at last. He hauled a big stick over to Turtle and stuck it under his shell.

He pushed a rock beneath the stick then he sprang up, grabbed hold, and swung.

"*Rock 'n' roll!*" cried Newt. Turtle wobbled, teetered on edge ...

and toppled over.

"Hooray!" shouted Turtle. "You *did* it!"

"That's what friends are for!" sang Newt.

Turtle stretched out his neck and gently nuzzled Newt. Newt's spots turned so dark they were almost purple.

The days were getting shorter. Ducks splashed off, chattering news of winter.

Newt licked a toe and held it up, testing the breeze. "Yep," he said. "Winter has finally come."

Turtle nodded with a drowsy smile.

"Well," said Newt, "it's nice knowing what we can do for each other."

"Yes," said Turtle wisely, "these things are worth remembering."

"Goodnight, Turtle," said Newt. "See you next spring!"

"Goodnight, Newt!" said Turtle.

And they slipped deep into the swamp mud, where it was snug and cosy and warm.

"Sleep tight!" murmured Turtle.

And that is what they did.

All winter.

Baby Bird

This is the bird that climbed out of the nest and …

flop
flop
flop …
he fell!

This is the squirrel that sniffed at the bird that fell.

This is the bee that buzzed round the bird that fell.

This is the frog that hopped over the bird that fell.

This is the cat that stalked the bird …

and fell himself (which was just as well).

by Joyce Dunbar
illustrated by Russell Ayto

This is the dog that opened wide and a bird that nearly walked inside.

A baby bird that wanted to fly up, up above, up above in the sky …
and thought he would have just one more try …

flap flap flap flap …

This is the bird that **flew**!

IN MY BATHROOM

by Carol Thompson

In my bathroom I can find all sorts of things:

a mirror

a bath mat

a tap

a toy

I go to the toilet.

I use the toilet roll

and pull the handle.

I have my bath with

my soap,

my sponge

and my duck.

I dry myself with
my towel.
I clean my teeth with
my toothbrush
and toothpaste.
I brush my hair with
my hairbrush
and comb.
I weigh
myself on
my bathroom
scales.
I get dressed
for bed in my
pyjamas and
dressing gown …
and I go to bed
clean and tidy!

COWBOY BABY

SUE HEAP

It was getting late and Sheriff Pa said, "Cowboy Baby, time for bed."

But Cowboy Baby wouldn't go to bed, not without Texas Ted and Denver Dog and Hank the Horse.

"Off you go and find them," said Sheriff Pa. "Bring them safely home."

Cowboy Baby put on his hat and his boots, and he set off on the trail of Texas Ted, Denver Dog and Hank the Horse. He went down the dusty path and through the barnyard gate.

Over by the hen-house he found ... **Texas Ted.**

"Howdy, Texas Ted," said Cowboy Baby.

Cowboy Baby and Texas Ted crossed the rickety bridge.

Down by the old wagon wheel they found ...

Denver Dog.

"Howdy, Denver Dog," said Cowboy Baby.

Cowboy Baby, Texas Ted and Denver Dog crawled through the long grass and out into the big, wide desert.

There by the little rock they found ...

Hank the Horse.

"Howdy, Hank the Horse," said Cowboy Baby.

"I'VE FOUND THEM," Cowboy Baby shouted to Sheriff Pa.

"That's dandy," Sheriff Pa called back. "Bring them home now, safe and sound."

Cowboy Baby and his gang sat down on the little rock. None of them wanted to go home.

"Let's hide!" said Cowboy Baby. "Hey, Sheriff Pa," he shouted. "I bet you can't find us, **NO SIRREE!**"

Sheriff Pa came to the big, wide desert.
"Shh!" said Cowboy Baby to his gang.
Sheriff Pa looked. He looked ... and he looked ... and he looked. But he couldn't find Cowboy Baby. No sirree!

"You got me beat, Cowboy Baby," called Sheriff Pa. "But if you come out, there'll be a big surprise, just for you!"
Out jumped Cowboy Baby. "Howdy, Sheriff Pa!"

The sheriff threw his lasso. It twisted and turned in the starlit sky and it caught ... a twinkling star.

"Look!" said Sheriff Pa, and he gave the star to Cowboy Baby.
"Now you're my deputy," he said.

Then Cowboy Baby picked up Texas Ted and Denver Dog and Hank the Horse, and Sheriff Pa picked up Cowboy Baby.

And all together they went home to bed.

"Nighty night, Cowboy Baby," said Sheriff Pa. But Cowboy Baby was already fast asleep.

YES SIRREE!

SOMETHING'S COMING!

by Richard Edwards • illustrated by Dana Kubick

"Something's coming!" said Elephant, sitting up.

"Nothing's coming," said Frog sleepily.

"Something's coming," said Elephant.

"Nothing's coming," said Little Rabbit.

"Something's coming," said Elephant.

"Nothing's coming," said Frog and Little Rabbit together.

"I'm sure something's coming," said Elephant.

Little Rabbit pushed back the blanket and looked out of the box.

"If Elephant thinks something's coming, we'll never get any sleep until we've found out what it is. Come on, let's have a look round."

And with the others following close behind, Little Rabbit climbed out of the box and dropped silently to the floor.

It was very quiet in the moonlit room.

They crept to the door and listened, but there was no sound of anything coming. They climbed on to the window-sill and peered out, but there was no sight of anything coming. They looked up the chimney. They looked in the cupboards. They looked under the sofa. They looked everywhere.

"See," said Little Rabbit. "Nothing's coming. Not a single thing."

Elephant raised his trunk. "Something's coming," he insisted. " I can feel it."

"Then what is it?" asked Frog.

"It's a ... It's a ...

It's a ... a ... a ...

TCHOO!"

And Elephant sneezed so hard that Frog and Little Rabbit went flying across the room and landed in a tangled heap in the corner.

"Is that what was coming?" asked Little Rabbit, picking herself up.

"Yes," said Elephant. "A ... a ... a ... a ... TCHOO!" And he sneezed again, even harder than before.

"I knew something was coming," said Elephant, breathing deeply through his nice clear trunk. "Let's go back to bed now."

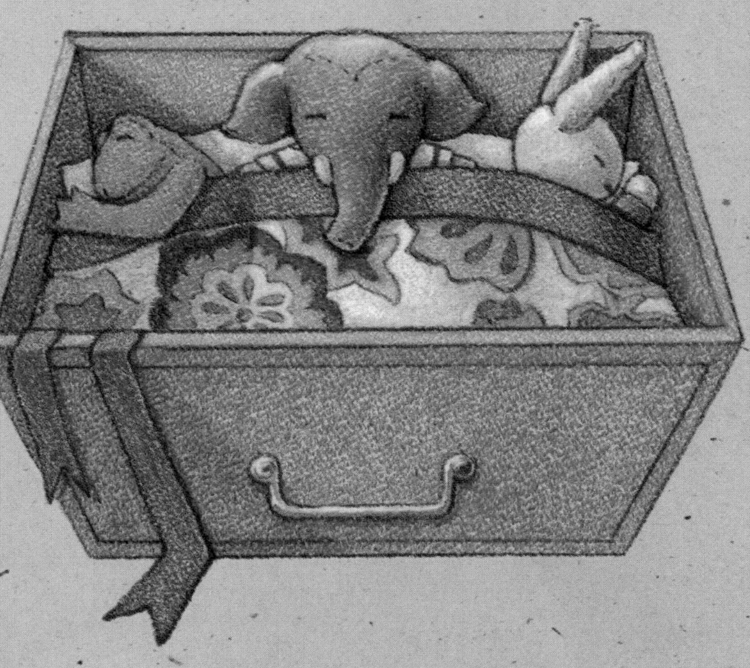

Soon they were fast asleep.

YOU AND ME, LITTLE BEAR

by
Martin Waddell
illustrated by
Barbara Firth

Once there were two bears, Big Bear and Little Bear. Big Bear is the big bear and Little Bear is the little bear.

Little Bear wanted to play, but Big Bear had things to do.
"I want to play!" Little Bear said.
"I've got to get wood for the fire," said Big Bear.
"I'll get some too," Little Bear said.
"You and me, Little Bear," said Big Bear. "We'll fetch the wood in together!"

"What shall we do now?" Little Bear asked.
"I'm going for water," said Big Bear.
"Can I come too?" Little Bear asked.
"You and me, Little Bear," said Big Bear. "We'll go for the water together."

"Now we can play," Little Bear said.
"I've still got to tidy our cave," said Big Bear.
"Well … I'll tidy too!" Little Bear said.
"You and me," said Big Bear. "You tidy your things, Little Bear. I'll look after the rest."

"I've tidied my things, Big Bear!" Little Bear said.
"That's good, Little Bear," said Big Bear. "But I'm not finished yet."
"I want you to play!" Little Bear said.
"You'll have to play by yourself, Little Bear," said Big Bear. "I've still got plenty to do!"

Little Bear went to play by himself, while Big Bear got on with the work.

Little Bear played bear-jump.
Little Bear played bear-slide. Little Bear played bear-swing. Little Bear played bear-tricks-with-bear-sticks. Little Bear played bear-stand-on-his-head and Big Bear came out to sit on his rock. Little Bear played bear-run-about-by-himself and Big Bear closed his eyes for a think.

Little Bear went to speak to Big Bear, but Big Bear was … asleep!
"Wake up, Big Bear!" Little Bear said. Big Bear opened his eyes. "I've played all my games by myself," Little Bear said.

Big Bear thought for a bit, then he said, "Let's play hide-and-seek, Little Bear."
"I'll hide and you seek," Little Bear said, and he ran off to hide.
"I'm coming now!" Big Bear called, and he looked till he found Little Bear. Then Big Bear hid, and Little Bear looked.

"I found you, Big Bear!" Little Bear said. "Now I'll hide again."

They played lots of bear-games. When the sun slipped away through the trees, they were still playing. Then Little Bear said, "Let's go home now, Big Bear."

Big Bear and Little Bear went home to their cave.
"We've been busy today, Little Bear!" said Big Bear.
"It was lovely, Big Bear," Little Bear said. "Just you and me playing ...

together."

Bathwater's Hot

by Shirley Hughes

Bathwater's hot,
  Seawater's cold,
Ginger's kittens are *very* young
  But Buster's getting old.

Some things you can throw away,
Some are nice to keep.
Here's someone who is wide awake,
Shhh, he's fast asleep!

Some things are hard as stone,
Some are soft as cloud.
Whisper very quietly…
SHOUT OUT LOUD!

It's fun to run very fast
Or to be slow.
The red light says 'stop'
And the green light says 'go'.

It's kind to be helpful,
Unkind to tease,
Rather rude to push and grab,
Polite to say 'please'.

Night time is dark,
Day time is light.
The sun says 'good morning'
And the moon says 'good night'.

Jonathan London

illustrated by
Patrick Benson

As the fire snaps
and roars
in the pot-belly stove,
my father snores,
but I can't sleep.
It was his idea
to come
to the north woods
where I've never
been before.

There are wolves
and bears out there.
And a lynx.

I hear a scratching
coming from
outside.

I get up,
creep to the door,
open it a crack,
then jump back ...

A WILDCAT!

The lynx steps in,
shakes first
one paw
then the other;
stands still
as a stone,
quiet as an owl,
in the middle
of the room.
Firelight glows
in its yellow eyes.

I shiver
in the warm room
as the lynx grows
and grows
and grows,
till its whiskers
touch the walls!

Great Lynx
commands
with his silence.

I grab fistfuls of fur
and climb up and up
on to the back
of the enormous cat.
And the next thing
I know ...

we're outside in
the snow!

Bunched like a fist
I clench fur as
Great Lynx creeps
on big cat's feet.
If I cry, my tears
will turn to ice.
In the trees
the moon trembles
on a bare
black branch,
then rolls
along with us
through the hard
northern night.

Great Lynx leaps
across
a frozen river,
steps across
glittering snow,
stalking some
invisible thing.
We climb a ridge
of ice and
there it is!

Great Lynx stops
and crouches.
And together
we watch the
dance of the
northern lights.

In an explosion
of snow
Great Lynx leaps
into the sky!
I cling to the
wildcat's back
as we claw
up and up
the curtains
of light ...
and land with
a pounce
on the big
round moon.

Suddenly
I'm filled with stars
and moonlight.

Great Lynx purrs
and if I could
I would purr too.

I yawn and
drowsily say,
"Lynx, let's go home!"

Down and down
we ripple
through the night,
down the curtains
of light ...
till we flop
like a pile of snow
before my cabin.

I climb off,
turn at the door.
Before my eyes
Great Lynx shrinks
down and down.

He crouches and
I feel his gaze
inside me
like fire
from
the northern lights.

He shakes a paw
and slowly
bounds away
through
the silent night.

The pot-belly's
still chugging.
My dad's
still snoring.

I curl up and
gaze at the fire.
As I close my eyes
and sink
into sleep,
I say ...

"Let the lynx
come in."

And the lynx
sleeps curled
in my dream
like the moon.